SAHAEL

THE INVASION OF KHARTOUM PALACE

SAHAEL, YOU WERE BEAUTIFUL YESTERDAY, AND SAFE.
NOW YOU BURN AT MY COMMAND.

YOUR KINGS ARE SLAIN.
RUN! ANYONE WHO CAN HEAR ME, RUN!
YOUR QUEENS CANNOT HELP YOU.

SAHAEL IS UNDER ATTACK! RUN!
YOUR PRINCESSES WILL DIE.

SAHAEL IS ON FIRE!
THE NARSANS AND THE ENNEAD HAVE INFILTRATED KHARTOUM PALACE.
THE NAVIGATORS ARE LIKELY DEAD. OTHER THAN THE GIRLS AND I, THERE WILL BE NO SURVIVORS. NATAS WILL MAKE SURE OF IT.
AND OUR HUSBANDS, THE KINGS?
DEAD. SLAUGHTERED BY NATAS!
I DO NOT UNDERSTAND ANY OF THIS. HOW COULD HE HAVE PENETRATED OUR DEFENSES SO EASILY?
THE HIGH KINGS OF SAHAEL WERE AS CHILDREN BEFORE HIM. OUR BLOODLINE MAY VERY WELL END TONIGHT.
NO!
WHAT OF MORRIGHAN?!
MORRIGHAN CAN TAKE CARE OF HERSELF, ALONG WITH HER DAUGHTER.
FOR NOW, WE MUST FIND A WAY TO KEEP OUR OWN CHILDREN SAFE.

LET US SPEAK WITHOUT SPEAKING, QUEEN SISTERS OF SAHAEL.
THE NABTAHENGE GATES HAVE ALREADY DESCENDED INTO THE CATACOMBS FOR SAFETY.
PORTAL MAGICS WILL NOT HELP US. OUR ESCAPE IS UP TO US NOW. NATAS IS HUNTING OUR DAUGHTERS.
ARE YOU CERTAIN? HOW CAN YOU BE SURE?
ALL THE ENNEAD AND NARSAN SOLDIERS RAN FOR THE GIRLS, NOT FOR ME OR OUR HUSBANDS.
NATAS LOOKED DIRECTLY AT OUR DAUGHTERS AS I RESCUED THEM. HE DIDN'T CARE ABOUT ME. HE CARED ABOUT THEM.
WHERE IS NATAS NOW?
NINTI, EXTEND YOUR SIGHT AND SEE THROUGH THE FOWL OVERHEAD.
PERHAPS YOU WILL SEE HIM.
GIVE ME A MOMENT.

I HAVE MADE CONTACT WITH A HAWK. I SEE THE FIRES. SOLDIERS ARE EVERYWHERE.
PEOPLE SCREAM BELOW. THE HAWK IS NERVOUS. THERE...
I SEE NATAS. HE IS ON THE PALACE STEPS. HE...
HE SAW ME. I FELT HIM. HE FELT ME. HE KNOWS WE'RE HERE. HE IS...
RAGE. AND POWER. MORE POWER THAN I'VE EVER FELT.
WE SHOULD LEAVE NOW, THROUGH THE PASSAGE AND INTO THE SEWERS. THE ANIMALS WILL PROTECT US IF I ASK.
NO!
WE MUST EVALUATE ALL OPTIONS FIRST. NATAS DID NOT PLAN THIS ASSAULT OVER BREAKFAST THIS MORNING.
WE CANNOT BE RASH IN OUR RESPONSE. NINTI, CAN YOU FLY THE GIRLS OUT OF HERE SAFELY?

THAT WON'T WORK! LORD COMMANDER NATAS WILL HAVE PLACED WIND LANCES OUTSIDE OF KHARTOUM PALACE JUST IN CASE OF AN ESCAPE ATTEMPT OF THIS TYPE.
IT IS A BASIC STRATEGY. THEY'D KILL ME AND THE GIRLS INSTANTLY.
NOT ONLY THAT, BUT I COULDN'T CARRY ALL THREE GIRLS. TWO PERHAPS, BUT NOT THREE.
I WOULDN'T BE ABLE TO FLY FOR LONG, OR VERY HIGH, WHILE CARRYING ALL OF THEM. WE WOULD MOST CERTAINLY BE SLAIN.
IT IS AS I FEARED. FOR OUR DAUGHTERS TO SAFELY ESCAPE, WE MAY HAVE TO PLACE THEM IN HARM'S WAY, AND OURSELVES ON THE PATH OF THE DEAD.
WHAT DO YOU MEAN?
I SAID WE MUST LOOK AT ALL OPTIONS, BUT IN MY HEART, I KNOW WHAT WE MUST DO. WE TAKE OUR DAUGHTERS TO THE SLAVE SHIPS. WE PASS THEM OFF AS SLAVES.
THEY WILL BE TAKEN TO OTHER LANDS IN AARDE, BUT OUR DEATHS WILL PROTECT THEM FROM HARM.

SLAVE PORTS? BETTER FOR THEM TO DIE WITH US THAN SPEND THEIR LIVES IN SLAVERY!
NO! AS NORMAL GIRLS, THEY'LL BLEND IN AT THE SLAVE PORTS ALONGSIDE THE OTHER ALKEBULAN CHILDREN. THIS WAY, OUR DAUGHTERS CAN EVADE LORD COMMANDER NATAS'S GRASP ENTIRELY.
I'D RATHER FIGHT AND DIE THAN ALLOW OUR DAUGHTERS TO SERVE AS SLAVES OR BE SOLD FOR THEIR FEMININE VIRTUES! THEY WERE CHOSEN AND BLESSED BY ISHTAR AND OBATALA.
I UNDERSTAND YOUR CONCERNS, BUT KEEP IN MIND THAT NEBIRIAU'S BRACELETS WILL PROVIDE THEM WITH PROTECTION IF WE EMPLOY THE PROPER SPELLS.
WITH OUR MAGICS, WE CAN GUARANTEE THEY WILL BE PROTECTED BY THE GODS.
IT IS NO SMALL THING I ASK OF YOU, MY SISTERS, BUT IF YOU WOULD RATHER DIE THAN SEE THEM SLAVES, WE CAN DIE NOW, THE THREE OF US, AND THEY CAN LIVE UNDER DIVINE PROTECTION UNTIL THEY ARE ABLE TO STAND ON THEIR OWN.
OUR LIVES IN EXCHANGE FOR THEIRS.
I AM PROPOSING A HOLY SACRIFICE. WE, MY QUEEN SISTERS...
WE ARE THE SACRIFICE.

OUR LIFE ENERGIES WILL FILL NEBIRIAU'S BRACELETS, AND NJIRU'S RINGS WILL ACT AS BARRIERS, ENSURING THE CHILDREN ARE NOT HARMED.
WHEN SOMEONE SEEKS TO HURT THEM, THE MAGICS WILL INFLUENCE THE PREDATOR'S MINDS TO MOVE ALONG.
OTHERS UNFORTUNATELY WILL TAKE OUR DAUGHTERS' PLACES AS A SACRIFICE FOR THE GREATER GOOD OF AARDE. AND IF WE MAKE THEIR EYES NORMAL LIKE AVERAGE ALKEBULANS, OUR GIRLS WILL BE PROTECTED FROM THE WORST OF A SLAVE'S FATE.
WHEN THE MAGIC IS NO MORE, A DEEP YEARNING WILL SPRING UP WITHIN THEM AND CALL OUR CHILDREN HOME.
THEIR EYES WILL BE BROWN? NO ONE WILL KNOW THEY ARE THE CHOSEN PRINCESSES?
YES. OUR LIVES...
OUR BLOOD, WILL ACT AS A PROTECTION TO THEM. IT IS THE ULTIMATE SACRIFICE OF A MOTHER TO SAVE HER DAUGHTER. ISHTAR AND OBATALA WILL LISTEN. SAHAEL WILL RISE ONCE MORE.
BUT WE WILL HAVE TO DIE. AND OUR DAUGHTERS WILL BECOME SLAVES, TRUSTED ONLY TO THE GODS FOR PROTECTION.
YES.

LORD COMMANDER! WE FOUND A PALACE SERVANT HIDING IN ONE OF THE KITCHENS.
I DON'T KNOW...
YOU SERVE THE KINGS AND QUEENS. THE KINGS ARE DEAD, AND THE QUEENS WILL SOON FOLLOW.
YOU NEED NOT SHARE THEIR FATE. IF YOU VALUE YOUR LIFE, YOU WILL TELL ME WHERE THEY ARE.
WHERE ARE THEY? YOU NEED NOT DIE WITH EVERYONE ELSE. I CAN BE MERCIFUL TO THOSE WHO SERVE ME.
I DON'T KNOW WHERE THEY ARE, BUT SEVERAL SECRET ROOMS EXIST, HIDDEN BY MAGIC.
ENNEAD LEGION! SEARCH THE PALACE! HAVE OUR PRIESTS FEEL FOR ANY REMNANTS OF MAGICAL MANIPULATION.

LORD COMMANDER! I HAVE DISCOVERED A WALL OFF THE MAIN CHAMBER THAT WAS RECENTLY TOUCHED BY THE ARTES OF THE ROYAL BLOODLINE.
SHOW ME.

LIFE MAGIC WILL KEEP ME ALIVE LONG ENOUGH TO HELP YOU ALL GET TO SAFETY. NATAS IS CLOSE.
I CAN FEEL HIM NEAR.
GO NOW INTO THE HIDDEN PASSAGE. MAY OUR SPIRITS MEET AGAIN BEFORE THE GODS OF SAHAEL.
OADIRA...
I LOVE YOU.

THOOM
HIGH QUEEN NERGAL.
I DIDN'T EXPECT TO FIND YOU BLEEDING TO DEATH IN A SECRET ROOM. WHERE ARE THE PRINCESSES?
NEVER... FIND...

I'M DISAPPOINTED IN YOU, HIGH QUEEN. AND YOUR HUSBAND. YOU ALL DIED SO...
POINTLESSLY. GIVE ME WHAT I WANT, AND YOUR PEOPLE DON'T NEED TO SUFFER FURTHER.
YOU LIE.

FIND THEM!
SHE WAS TRYING TO STALL US. THEY CAN'T HAVE GOTTEN FAR!
SEARCH THE FOREST WITH THE MASTIFFS.

FOLLOW THE RATS. I'M COMMUNICATING WITH THEM. THEY WILL LEAD US TO SAFETY.
THE RATS FLEE NATAS THE SAME AS ALL LIVING CREATURES SHOULD.
SPIDERS!
FEAR NOT. WE ARE SAFE. THE ARANAK SPIDER'S BITE IS NOT DEADLY.

I SENSE ANIMAL LIFE ALL AROUND, SCARED. THERE IS A CAVE UP AHEAD.
SOME SAHAELIAN BEARS HAVE TAKEN REFUGE THERE. THEY ARE CONFUSED.

YOU ARE AFRAID, BEAR OF SAHAEL.
I SENSE YOUR NAME IS OLAMI.

YOU HAVE SEEN MUCH THIS DAY, OLAMI.
SHOW ME WHAT YOU'VE SEEN. SHOW ME WHAT THE ANIMALS SEE NOW.

THE ENNEAD ARE DRAWING NEARER. ALL LIFE IN THE FOREST IS AFRAID.
THE TIME FOR MY SACRIFICE HAS ARRIVED. MY LIFE FORCE WILL ENSURE THE SURVIVAL AND PROTECTION OF OUR DAUGHTERS.
WE KNEW WE WOULD NOT SURVIVE THIS JOURNEY, AAMIRA?
YES, MAMA?
OUR TEARS WILL DO LITTLE FOR US NOW, MY SWEET LOVE.
WHAT I'M ABOUT TO ASK OF YOU WILL BE THE HARDEST THING YOU'LL EVER DO. TAKE THIS BLADE. I WILL GUIDE YOUR HAND. DON'T BE AFRAID, SIMPLY TRUST IN ME, AND THE GODS OF OUR ANCESTORS.

THIS WOUND WILL ALLOW ME TO BLEED OUT SLOWLY WHILE I PASS MY PROTECTIVE POWER ONTO YOUR BRACELET. IT WILL ALSO GIVE ME ENOUGH TIME TO SEND ANIMALS IN DIFFERENT DIRECTIONS TO CONFUSE OUR ENEMIES.
YOU NEED TO GET AWAY FROM LORD COMMANDER NATAS.
I HAVE THE STRONGEST CONNECTION WITH THE ALPHA BEAR. HIS NAME IS OLAMI. HE WILL BE YOUR MOUNT, MY SWEET CHILD.
WHY DID IT HAVE TO COME TO THIS?
SO, MY SISTER. GET THEM TO THE BOATS.
LET OUR STRENGTH PROTECT THEM. TRUST IN OUR LAND AND THE GODS OF OUR ANCESTORS. SAHAEL WILL RISE ONCE MORE. NATAS WILL NOT TRIUMPH FOR LONG.

OVER HERE! WE'VE FOUND FOOTPRINTS!
CALL LORD...
BY THE GODS!
GRUAHG!
KILL THEM!
KILL THE BEARS!

GRAUU

QUEEN REGENT ARISHKEGAL, I FOUND HIGH QUEEN NERGAL BLEEDING FROM THE THROAT AT KHARTOUM.
NOW HERE YOU ARE IN A SIMILAR STATE. WHAT MAGICS ARE YOU PLAYING WITH?
NOTHING...
A MAN LIKE YOU WOULD...
UNDERSTAND, DEMON-MADE-FLESH.
I AM FAR MORE THAN ANY DEMON, MY QUEEN.
YOUR DEATH WILL MEAN NOTHING, JUST LIKE THE DEATH OF YOUR HUSBAND. HE SPOKE YOUR NAME AS I CRUSHED HIS HEAD BENEATH MY BOOT.

THEN YOU CAN BE CRUSHED AS WELL!

WHAT ARE YOU QUEENS UP TO? WHY ARE YOU GIVING YOUR LIVES IN SUCH A WAY?
YOU WILL NOT KEEP MY PRIZE FROM ME!

THEY'VE BEEN HEADING EAST TOWARD THE HARBOR. RIDE HARD!
WE MUST ARRIVE BEFORE THE PRINCESSES CAN ESCAPE!

STAY CLOSE, DAUGHTERS.
NATAS'S ARMY MUST HAVE ARRIVED YESTERDAY AND TAKEN THE PORT BEFORE WE EVEN KNEW THE ATTACK WAS TAKING PLACE.

EVERYONE THEY HAVEN'T KILLED THEY'RE TAKING CAPTIVE AS SLAVES. THIS IS WORSE THAN I IMAGINED.

HEZIARA, DAUGHTER, COME HERE. I WISH I COULD FLY US ALL OUT OF HERE, BUT I CAN'T CARRY EVERYONE.
JUST AS HIGH QUEEN NERGAL AND QUEEN REGENT ARISHKEGAL, THE TIME FOR MY SACRIFICE HAS COME.
MY WINGS WOULD GIVE OUT BEFORE I GOT EVEN A HUNDRED FEET IN THE AIR, AND THEIR WIND-LANCES WOULD KILL US INSTANTLY.
IT'S TIME FOR YOU TO CUT MY WRISTS. DO IT NOW, HEZIARA! LET MY BLOOD SEAL THE SPELL AND PROTECT YOU UNTIL YOUR TIME OF POWER HAS COME.
I CAN'T MAMA!
I DON'T WANT TO!
YOU CAN. YOU MUST BE BRAVE.

LIKE MY QUEEN SISTERS, LET MY SACRIFICE SEAL OUR BARGAIN.
MAY THE GODS WATCH OVER AND PROTECT YOU, DAUGHTERS OF SAHAEL.
YOU APPEAR NOW AS AVERAGE CHILDREN WITH AVERAGE EYES. NO GLOWING TATTOOS MARK YOUR SKIN OR WINGS TO DRAW ATTENTION.
NO ONE WILL KNOW YOU CAME FROM THE SEED OF HIGH QUEENS AND GLORIOUS KINGS OF SAHAEL.
WHEN THE TIME COMES, YOU WILL BE CALLED BACK AS SAVIORS OF OUR PEOPLE AND LAND.

YOUR PROTECTION IS IN PLACE. NOW...
I HAVE...
ONE MORE ARTE TO...
PERFORM. GO AT MY SIGNAL.

WHAT DEVILRY IS THIS MIST?

ME EYES! IT'S PECKIN' ME EYES!

GO, DAUGHTERS OF...
SAHAEL.
THE KORI BUSTARDS WILL LEAD YOU TO THE SHIPS. KEEP THEM...
SAFE, MY FLYING BROTHERS.

BY SOLOMON AND THE SEERS OF OLD!
ARE THOSE...
LOOK AT THEIR HAIR! FADED, BUT...
THEIR EYES DON'T GLOW! IS IT REALLY...?
THE SACRED BLOOD LIVES!
HIDE THEM! KEEP THEM SAFE NOW!
SPLIT THEM UP BEFORE THE MIST DISSIPATES!
DON'T LET THE GUARDS SEE.
DON'T BE FRIGHTENED. I WORKED IN THE PALACE FOR MANY YEARS BEFORE RETIRING TO THE FISHING REALMS HERE ON THE RIVER.
I SERVE THE KINGS AND QUEENS EVEN NOW AS A HUMBLE FISHERMAN. YOU ARE SAFE, YOUNG ONE. THE SACRED BLOOD WILL LIVE ON. WE WILL MAKE SURE OF IT.
SAHAEL HAS NOT FALLEN SO LONG AS YOU AND YOUR SISTER PRINCESS BREATHE.

LORD COMMANDER!
WE'VE SEARCHED THE DOCKS. WE'VE FOUND ONE OF THE QUEENS BLEEDING UNDER A NEARBY TREE.
SHOW ME, COMMANDER NORG.
ANOTHER BLEEDING QUEEN.
YOU'VE DONE SOMETHING. WHERE ARE THE PRINCESSES?!?
THEY ARE GONE...
SAFELY OUT OF YOUR REACH. SAHAEL WILL NOW...
DIE WITH ME.
I WILL FIND THEM.
EK SAL JOU IN DIE HEL SIEN!

SPLASH

FIND THE PRINCESSES NOW! FOUR YOUNG GIRLS, POTENTIALLY WITH THE REMAINING QUEEN!
PAY ATTENTION TO THE PRINCESSES EYES! THEY'LL DIFFER FROM THE REST.
SEARCH EVERY CHILD! BRING THEM TO ME! REMOVE EVERYONE FROM THE SHIPS!
THE DAUGHTERS MUST BE FOUND. THERE CAN BE NO REMNANT.
MY REVENGE IS INCOMPLETE IF THE PRINCESSES SURVIVE.
I WILL NOT FAIL.
SO CLOSE!
AT LAST, I HAVE GROUND THE CHOSEN BLOODLINE TO DUST.

LORD COMMANDER! WE SEARCHED THE SHIPS.
THERE ARE NO CHILDREN WITH EYES OF THE CHOSEN BLOODLINE.
MANY HAVE COLORED HAIR COMMON IN THE CAPITAL, BUT NONE WITH EYES THAT GLOW WITH THE ETERNAL FLAME.

WE ARE THWARTED... FOR NOW.
WHAT IS HAPPENING TO THE WATER OF THE POND AND THE GRASS?
AS WAS PROPHESIED, GENERAL COMMANDER NORG. LOOK AT THE SKIES. THE MOMENT QUEEN NINTI DIED, THE AIR GREW INCREASINGLY TOXIC.
THE BIRDS, CRITTERS, EVEN THE FISH ARE FLEEING SAHAEL WITH HASTE.
WE'VE EITHER ENSLAVED OR COMPLETELY ERADICATED SAHAEL'S FOUR KINGDOMS, INCLUDING KHARTOUM PALACE.

SAHAEL'S SECONDARY DEFENSES WILL EXTERMINATE ANY IN HIDING. THIS PROVES THE PRINCESSES ARE NO LONGER IN CONTACT WITH THE LAND OF SAHAEL.

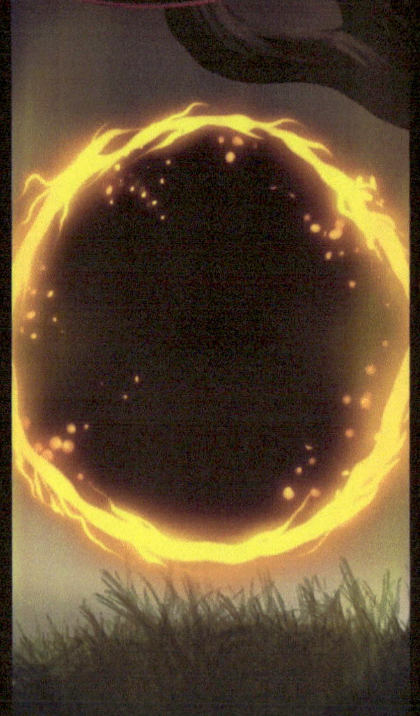

THEY ARE GONE BUT WILL BE FOUND. I GO TO NAHARIS'S REALM FOR A SEASON.

I WILL CONTACT YOU WHEN THE SIGNS OF THE TIMES ARE CLEARER. SELL THE SLAVES IN LONDONE AND CONTACT ME IF ANY WORD REACHES YOUR EARS REGARDING THE FOUR PRINCESSES.

THE LAND OF SAHAEL DIES! LOOK!
THE PROPHECIES ARE TRUE! THE CHOSEN BLOODLINE IS DEAD!

THE BLOODLINE IS NOT DEAD, CHILD. ONE DAY, YOU WILL HELP US RETURN HOME.

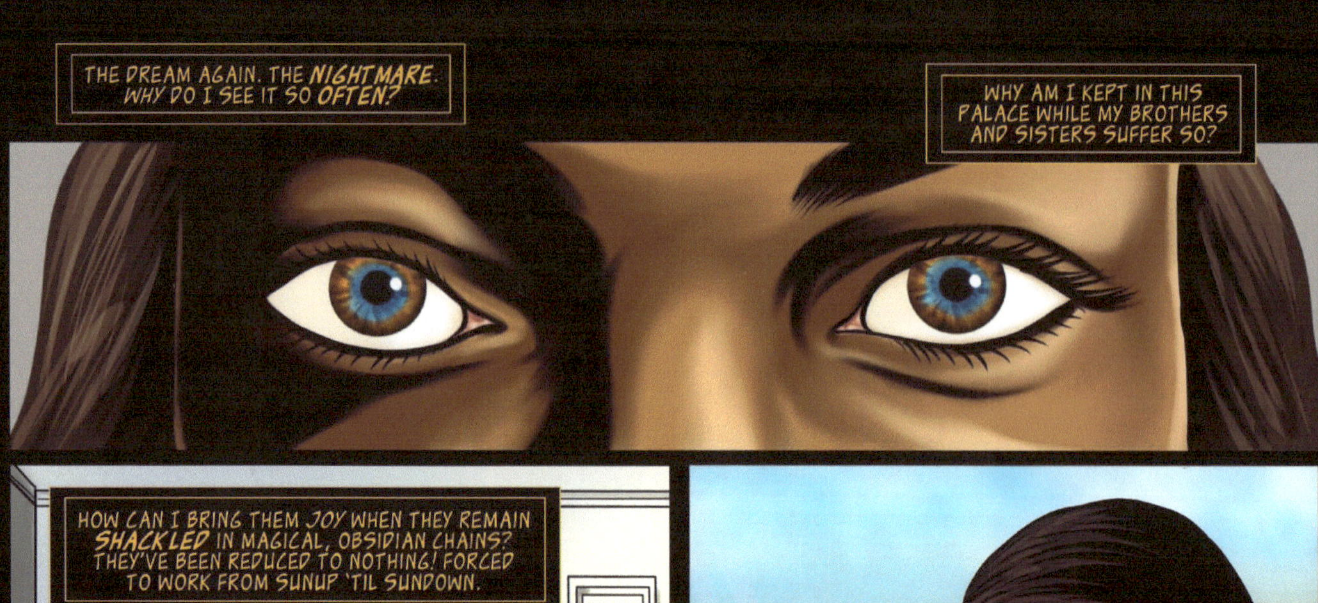
THE DREAM AGAIN. THE NIGHTMARE. WHY DO I SEE IT SO OFTEN?
WHY AM I KEPT IN THIS PALACE WHILE MY BROTHERS AND SISTERS SUFFER SO?

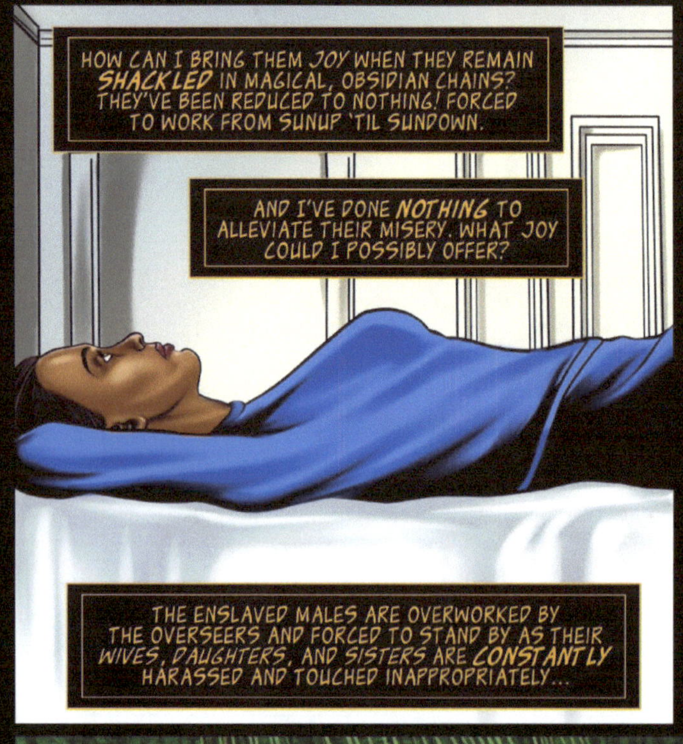
HOW CAN I BRING THEM JOY WHEN THEY REMAIN SHACKLED IN MAGICAL, OBSIDIAN CHAINS? THEY'VE BEEN REDUCED TO NOTHING! FORCED TO WORK FROM SUNUP 'TIL SUNDOWN.
AND I'VE DONE NOTHING TO ALLEVIATE THEIR MISERY. WHAT JOY COULD I POSSIBLY OFFER?
THE ENSLAVED MALES ARE OVERWORKED BY THE OVERSEERS AND FORCED TO STAND BY AS THEIR WIVES, DAUGHTERS, AND SISTERS ARE CONSTANTLY HARASSED AND TOUCHED INAPPROPRIATELY...

RAPED AND MOLESTED BY THESE EVIL WITANS, WHO LOOK AT ME AND WANT TO DIG THEIR CLAWS INTO ME.
GET BACK TO IT, SAHAELIAN NIGGERS!
BUT THEY NEVER DO! AM I CURSED TO BE SAFE WHILE I WATCH THOSE AROUND ME SUFFER?

OADIRA! GET DRESSED. THE CARRIAGE IS ALMOST READY TO GO. THE MADAME WILL BE ANGRY. YOUR SLEEPING IN LATE WON'T DO TODAY. DID YOU SNEAK OUT AGAIN LAST NIGHT?
I HAD TO, AMAHLÉ!
SEVERAL OF THE LITTLE BOYS WERE GOING TO BE LEFT IN THE PEN ALL NIGHT BECAUSE THEY WERE PLAYING INSTEAD OF WORKING. IT'S SO COLD THIS TIME OF YEAR! I HAD TO GET THEM TO THEIR FAMILIES.
I UNDERSTAND, BUT YOU NEED TO GET READY. MADAME LALAURIE WANTS YOU IN THE CARRIAGE AND ON THE WAY TO THE ROYAL RUMBLE WITHIN THE HALF HOUR.
I STILL CAN'T BELIEVE SHE'S SELLING YOUR VIRTUE TO THE RUMBLE CHAMPION.
I WON'T LET IT COME TO THAT, I'LL ESCAPE IF I HAVE TO.
THE MADAME IS BEING BLACKMAILED, OADIRA! NO ONE IS SAFE. YOUR SISTERS WILL BE THERE TOO. A LOT OF MONEY WILL BE CHANGING HANDS.
OVERLORDS WILL BE WATCHING YOU CLOSELY EVERY SECOND. JUST BE CAREFUL, WHATEVER YOU CHOOSE, AND IF YOU CAN, COME BACK TO US, PRINCESS OF SAHAEL.

"PRINCESS OF SAHAEL." SOME OF THE SLAVES CALL ME THAT, BUT IT'S A FANTASY.
IT'S LIKE WHEN THEY SAY WE'LL BE FREE SOMEDAY. I DON'T BELIEVE IT.
IN MY NIGHTMARE I REMEMBER A PALACE AND A QUEEN.
I REMEMBER A SLIT THROAT AND BLOOD EVERYWHERE.
THEN I REMEMBER WATCHING MY PEOPLE SUFFER EVERY DAY SINCE, WHILE I'M CARED FOR LIKE A FATTENED CALF WAITING FOR THE RIGHT BUYER.
WHAT AM I? A PRINCESS OF DIRT. A PRINCESS OF NOTHING.
YOU ALMOST MADE US LATE, OADIRA!
I'M SORRY, MADAME LALAURIE. IT WAS NOT MY INTENT TO MAKE YOU WAIT.
KNOW YOUR PLACE, NIGGER BITCH. YOU WANT TO LOOK ME IN THE EYE, YOU DO IT WITH SOME GODDAMN HUMILITY FOR MY GRACE AND KINDNESS TOWARD YOU. I COULD HAVE PUT YOU OUT WITH THE WHORES IF I'D WANTED.
SIT UP STRAIGHT!
ESCAPE AND DIE

MADAME LALAURIE.
I HATE HER. I HATE EVERYTHING ABOUT THIS PLACE, THIS CITY, THESE SHIPS, THESE PEOPLE.
I WELCOME YOU AND YOUR PROPERTY TO LONDONE HARBOR.
THANK YOU FOR YOUR SERVICE, SOLDIER.
I HAVE BEEN ASKED TO ESCORT YOU TO THE SHIP.
YOU WERE ORIGINALLY SLATED TO SAIL ON THE NIGHTINGALE... BUT WORD OF YOUR ARRANGEMENT WITH THE POTENTIAL CHAMPION OF THE RUMBLE HAS REACHED LORD COMMANDER NATAS'S EARS.
HE INVITES YOU TO SAIL ON HIS PERSONAL YACHT.
NATAS? HIS NAME IS WHISPERED LIKE A DEMON FROM HELL BY THE SLAVES.
HE WAS A NIGHTMARE OF THE PAST; A PRESENCE IN THE SHADOWS ONLY. THERE MUST BE SOME MISTAKE.
LORD COMMANDER NATAS? HAS HE RETURNED TO AARDE?
HE HAS, MADAME.
MADAME LALAURIE, I PRESUME.

LORD COMMANDER NATAS!
WHAT A...
SURPRISE!
THE WORLD BURNS. A MAN WITH RED EYES SMILES. NATAS CONQUERED SAHAEL 15 YEARS AGO. I'VE NEVER MET HIM BEFORE...
I'VE FEARED HIM SINCE CHILDHOOD.
NEVER EVEN SEEN HIM BEFORE, AND YET RIGHT NOW IT FEELS LIKE I'VE KNOWN HIM SINCE CHILDHOOD...
MADAME LALAURIE, I AM TOLD YOU WILL BE PRESENTING SOME VIRGINS TO OUR BULLS AT THE RUMBLE. WHAT A BLESSING FOR OUR WARRIORS.
I WOULD INVITE YOU TO LEAVE YOUR SLAVE BELOW DECK WHILE YOU JOIN US FOR LUNCH.
I WOULD BE HONORED, LORD NATAS.

YOUR HAIR COLOR IS UNIQUE, DAUGHTER. FEW SAHAELIANS ENJOY SUCH SHADES NATURALLY.
A PITY YOUR EYES DO NOT MATCH.
MADAME LALAURIE, I THINK YOU WILL ENJOY OUR LUNCH. MY SLAVES HAVE BEEN TRAINED IN ALOE PORT BY THE MOST RENOWNED...
HE CALLED ME "DAUGHTER". THE WORD ITSELF FEELS DIRTY NOW. I DON'T KNOW HIM, BUT I HATE HIM.
I HATE HIM EVERY BIT AS MUCH AS I HATE LALAURIE. MY STOMACH TWISTS. I CAN'T HOLD IT IN.

TWO DAYS LATER.
OADIRA! SISTER!
HEZIARA AND AAMIRA! MY COUSINS AND SPIRITUAL SISTERS.
LET US SPEAK WITHOUT SPEAKING, SISTERS.
YOU LOOK WELL OADIRA. WE WERE AFRAID WE WOULDN'T SEE YOU.
MADAME LALAURIE AND HER SISTERS ARE BEING BLACKMAILED.
WE WILL BE SOLD TO THE RUMBLE CHAMPION FOR BREEDING RIGHTS!
I KNOW. I HAVE A PLAN. AFTER THE RUMBLE WE WILL BE TAKEN TO THE VICTOR'S TENT TO BE EXAMINED BY THE MATRONS. FROM THERE WE MAKE A RUN FOR IT.
WE WON'T MAKE IT! THERE ARE TOO MANY GUARDS.
I DON'T CARE, SO LONG AS THE TWO OF YOU ARE WITH ME.
I HAVEN'T SEEN THEM IN THREE YEARS, NOT SINCE WE WERE BROUGHT TO THE RUMBLE TOGETHER WHEN WE WERE 15.
THEY LOOK HEALTHY AND STRONG. STRONG ENOUGH TO ESCAPE WITH ME? I PRAY SO.

ENJOY IT WHILE IT LASTS, YOU BITCHES WILL MEET YOUR BULL SOON ENOUGH.
GIVE THE GIRLS A MOMENT, MARTHA.
THEY COULD BE HAVING MORE THAN A MOMENT IF YOU HADN'T KILLED THAT BASTARD HUSBAND OF YOURS A DECADE AGO AND BEEN SMART ENOUGH TO CLEAN UP YOUR DAMN MESS.
AND PERHAPS IF YOUR THIRD HUSBAND HAD REWRITTEN HIS WILL LIKE HE TOLD YOU HE DID BEFORE HE 'ACCIDENTALLY' FELL FROM THE BALCONY, WE'D HAVE ENOUGH MONEY TO WEATHER THE STORM, WOULDN'T WE, LITTLE SISTER?
MATRONS AND HONORED GUESTS, LET US ENTER THE ARENA FOR THE ANNUAL EVENT.
PRESIDENT TIBERIUS WILL BE SITTING WITH US, AS WILL HIS GENERALS.
BLACKMAIL IS A DIRTY MESS, SISTERS. AT LEAST WE HAVE SOME ASSETS WE CAN PART WITH. IT WAS GOING TO HAPPEN SOONER OR LATER ANYWAY. THAT'S WHY WE BOUGHT THEM.
COME! WE DON'T WANT TO KEEP THE SUITORS

WE NEED TO CONTINUE PLAYING ALONG UNTIL AN OPPORTUNITY PRESENTS ITSELF THAT WE CAN TAKE ADVANTAGE OF. I FEEL LIKE ISHTAR AND THE SEERS OF OLD WILL GUIDE US IN OUR FLIGHT.
I'VE BEEN PLANNING MY ESCAPE FOR THE PAST WEEKS AS WELL, EVER SINCE I FOUND OUT ABOUT THE MADAME'S PLAN. I COULDN'T DO IT ALONE.
I WANTED YOU BOTH BESIDE ME. NOW I WANT OUR PEOPLE BESIDE ME TOO. I PRAY FOR THEIR SALVATION.
ONCE WE'RE SOLD OFF AND MARRIED TO ONE OF THESE BRUTES, THERE'S NO WAY TO KNOW HOW OUR LIVES WILL UNFOLD.
IT WON'T COME TO THAT. WE WILL BE FREE. OUR PEOPLE WILL BE FREE. TRUST IN THAT.
I ONCE SAID I DIDN'T BELIEVE WE'D EVER BE FREE. I'D LIKE TO SAY THAT'S CHANGED. IT HASN'T.
WE VERY WELL MAY DIE TRYING TO ESCAPE TONIGHT, AND I'M FINE WITH THAT. DEATH WILL BE ENOUGH.

LADIES AND GENTLEMEN! WELCOME TO THE FIFTIETH ANNUAL ROYAL RUMBLE! A SPECTACLE LIKE NO OTHER! THE BIGGEST, STRONGEST, AND BADDEST OF BULLS HAVE COME HERE TO ACHIEVE VICTORY OVER ALL RIVALS!
THIS YEAR, IN COMMEMORATION OF OUR 50TH RUMBLE, WE HAVE A FULL 50 WRESTLERS COMPETING FOR THE PRIZE. I'D LIKE TO OFFER A SPECIAL ROUND OF APPLAUSE FOR LAST YEAR'S CHAMPION, DEMARCO, AS HE RETURNS TO SHOW HIS DOMINANCE!
THIS ISN'T ABOUT A MATTER OF PRIDE, DEAR SPECTATORS. THESE BRAVE AND POWERFUL MEN COMPETE FOR BREEDING RIGHTS AND THEIR CHOICE OF WOMEN. WOULDN'T WE ALL WANT THAT PRIVILEGE?
THEY FIGHT HERE NOW FOR PLEASURE LATER, AND TO CREATE THE NEXT GENERATION OF FIGHTERS. IT'S AN OPPORTUNITY TO ENJOY THE SPOILS OF THEIR HARD WORK FOR THE NEXT TWELVE MONTHS IN HOPES OF ONE DAY COMPETING FOR THEIR FREEDOM!
THE RUMBLE PROVIDES THESE WRESTLERS A PLACE OF SOLACE AND COMFORT; AN ESCAPE FROM THE CRUELTIES OF AARDE. THIS IS A MERCY FOR THEM. REMEMBER, WHAT I'VE DONE FOR YOU YOUR WHOLE LIFE, AND WHAT I DO TODAY, IS A MERCY.

DING DING DING DING
LET THE BATTLE COMMENCE!

THAT WAS A RUTHLESS MOVE FROM NEZIKIAH!
HE WAS TRANSPORTED ON THE SLAVE SHIPS FROM SAHAEL ITSELF, WITH THE STRENGTH AND FEROCITY OF HIS SAVAGE BLOODLINE!
AND LOOK AT DEMARCO!
HE JUST SHATTERED THAT POOR BULL'S FEMUR!
I HATE THIS. NOTHING BUT DESPERATE MEN KILLING EACH OTHER FOR THE ENTERTAINMENT OF WITANS. IT'S SICK.

TWO HOURS LATER.
NEZIKIAH AND DEMARCO, BOTH BRUISED AND BLOODY, FIGHT AS THE LAST TWO WRESTLERS.
IT'S BEEN A LONG MATCH, BUT ONLY TWO FIGHTERS REMAIN: NEZIKIAH AND DEMARCO!
SUCH BRUTALITY! LOOK AT THAT SKILL! THAT FEROCITY!
WHAT AN UPSET! DEMARCO, THE REIGNING CHAMPION, HAS BEEN DEFEATED!
I DON'T EVEN SEE HIM SURFACING!
NEZIKIAH WINS!
NEZIKIAH WINS!
TWO BEASTS COMPETING FOR THE RIGHT TO PROCREATE!
NEZIKIAH IT IS. FOLLOW ME, GIRLS, TO THE TENT OF HIS TRAINER. YOU WILL BE TREATED WELL, I PROMISE.

IT SEEMS YOU WERE RIGHT. I WONDERED HOW YOU WERE SO CONFIDENT IN YOUR VICTORY, BUT NOW IT SEEMS IT WAS INEVITABLE. YOUR WRESTLER DELIVERED AGAINST ALL ODDS.
IT IS UNORTHODOX...
BUT AS LONG AS PAYMENT IS BEING MADE, WE'LL ALLOW IT. COME SISTERS, LET US GIVE THEM SOME...
PRIVACY.
AS HAS BEEN ARRANGED BY THE RUMBLE REGENTS, YOUR BULL WILL BE GIVEN ACCESS TO MY FAMILY'S THREE VIRGINS ON OUR ESTATES IN LUCEDALE, VANNADALE, AND ABINGDALE.
THESE THREE YOUNG WOMEN ARE THE LALAURIE FAMILY'S PUREST PRIZED VIRGINS.
LOOK AT THEIR TEETH; PERFECT AND WHITE. THAT ALONE PROVES THEIR HEALTH AND
THEIR HEALTH WAS NEVER IN DOUBT. THE PAYMENT IS BEING MADE RIGHT NOW AS AGREED UPON.
NOW IS OUR CHANCE, COUSINS. ALL WE NEED IS AN EXCUSE TO STEP OUTSIDE FOR A MOMENT AND WE CAN RUN. I DON'T CARE IF WE DIE. I WON'T BE GIVEN TO SOME ANIMAL WHO KILLS FOR SPORT.
IF YOU WANT TO RUN, BY ALL MEANS, RUN. BUT I DO WISH YOU WOULD HEAR WHAT I HAVE TO SAY BEFORE YOU MAKE ANY RASH DECISIONS.
WOULD YOU MIND, MADAME LALAURIE, IF I SPOKE WITH THESE YOUNG WOMEN ALONE BEFORE THEY ARE INSPECTED BY THE MATRONS?
I WOULD LIKE THEM TO MEET NEZIKIAH WITHOUT PRYING EYES.

HOW DID YOU DO THAT? WHO ARE YOU?
I AM SOLOMON, KEEPER OF HISTORIES, AND PROTECTOR OF SAHAEL.
IT HAS TAKEN A LOT OF PATIENCE AND TIME TO FIND ALL THREE OF YOU. IT WASN'T TO GET YOU ALL IN ONE LOCATION, EITHER.
I HAVE EMPLOYED THOUSANDS OF RUNAWAY SLAVES, RUNAWAYS THAT ESCAPED YOUR RESPECTIVE PLANTATIONS AND ESTATES, TO SHARE WITH ME INFORMATION ABOUT YOUR WHEREABOUTS IN THE COLONIES.
MY EDUCATORS HAVE DONE A WONDERFUL JOB TO GET YOU ALL HERE.
WHAT DO YOU MEAN, 'GET US HERE?'
WE WERE BROUGHT BY OUR MISTRESSES. THEY OWE A DEBT, AND WE ARE THE PRICE.
AND WHO DO YOU THINK WAS BLACKMAILING THE LALAURIE SISTERS?
SURPRISED? LET ME MAKE A FEW GUESSES, SHALL I?
YOUR BRACELETS HAVE BEEN GLOWING MORE FREQUENTLY LATELY.
YOU MAY HAVE NOTICED YOUR EYES GLOWING AS WELL.
AND YOU'VE BEEN HAVING VIVID NIGHTMARES. THE SIGNS OF THE TIMES ARE UPON US.

YOU THREE ARE PRINCESSES OF SAHAEL. YOU MUST UNDERSTAND THE SACRED KNOWLEDGE AND INTRICACIES OF YOUR ANCIENT BLOOD LINEAGES FROM THE BEGINNING.
THERE IS A LOT THE THREE OF YOU WILL UNLEARN AS WHITE SUPREMACY HAS POLLUTED AND CORRUPTED YOUR MINDS.
I WILL START BY TELLING YOU WHO YOU TRULY ARE: KEMITES FROM THE LAST OF THE ANCIENT BLOODLINES.
YOUR ANCESTORS ARRIVED IN AARDE INSIDE OF AN ORICHALCUM-MADE VESSEL THAT TRAVERSED THE UNIVERSE DISGUISED AS AN ASTEROID.
WHEN THE VESSEL ARRIVED HERE IT BROKE INTO TWELVE PIECES IN THE ATMOSPHERE, WITH THE MAIN PIECE CRASHING IN THE CENTER OF ALKEBULAN.
THEY WERE THE FIRST PEOPLE TO INHABIT AARDE.
ORICHALCUM IS AN ETERNAL MINERAL WITH PROPERTIES BEYOND WHAT AARDE WAS EVER MEANT TO SUSTAIN.
THEY NAMED THE CONTINENT ALKEBULAN, MEANING THE MOTHERLAND. SAHAEL BECAME ITS CAPITAL NATION.

FOR A MILLENNIA THERE WAS PEACE, AS THE RULERS OF THE NATION OF SAHAEL TAUGHT THE OTHER PEOPLES OF AARDE ABOUT SCIENCE, NAVIGATION, AND AGRICULTURE.
BUT THEN CAME NATAS, THE FALLEN ANGEL AND SELFISH DESTROYER.
HE WANTED BODIES FOR HIS SPIRIT FOLLOWERS FROM THE HIGHER REALMS. HE CORRUPTED THE NATIONS WITH WHITE DARKNESS, TEACHING HATE AND BIGOTRY.
WHEN YOU WERE CHILDREN, HE CONQUERED SAHAEL WITH POWER EVEN I WAS UNFAMILIAR WITH.
WHERE HE RECEIVED HIS STRENGTH, I CANNOT GUESS.

HE CAME WITH VENGEANCE TO WIPE OUT THE ONLY PEOPLE WHO COULD STAND IN HIS WAY.

HE BLAMES ALL LIFE FOR HIS MISTAKES, AND CARES ONLY FOR HIS DISEMBODIED FOLLOWERS.

BUT THE FOUR OF YOU WERE CHOSEN TO RIGHT ALL THOSE WRONGS.
IT WAS PROPHESIED. YOUR BLOODLINES ARE DESTINED TO RESHAPE AARDE IN THE IMAGE IT WAS ORIGINALLY SUPPOSED TO BE.
WITAN BEAUTY IS BUILT ON THE BACKS OF SLAVES PICKING COTTON, HARVESTING TOBACCO, AND MINING OBSIDIAN ORE.
AN AARDE FREE OF WITAN PERSECUTION WILL ALLOW PEOPLE OF COLOR THE ABILITY TO THRIVE
YOUR POWERS WILL NEED DEVELOPMENT IF YOU ARE TO BE READY WHEN THE TIME COMES.
THERE IS A FOURTH PRINCESS WHO ESCAPED SAHAEL'S DESTRUCTION AS WELL, DAMISIAH. SHE WILL JOIN YOU WHEN THE TIME IS RIGHT.
UNTIL THEN, EVERY SAHAELIAN, EVERY PERSON BORN WITH DARK SKIN, WILL BE VULNERABLE TO THE CRUELTIES OF THE NARSANS WHO WANT TO SPREAD WHITE SUPREMACY ALL OVER AARDE.
EVERYTHING DEPENDS ON ALL FOUR OF YOU PRINCESSES GETTING BACK TO SAHAEL. UNTIL YOU DO, AARDE WILL CONTINUE TO BE OUT OF BALANCE.

WHAT POWERS? I DON'T HAVE ANY POWERS.
YOU DO, AND YOU WILL. YOU'RE NOT CHILDREN OR POWERLESS SLAVES, YOU ARE OF KEMETTIAN ROYALTY.
YOU ARE QUEENS. YOU HAVE NATURAL AND DEFIANT CONFIDENCE. YOU HAVE BEEN PROTECTED AND WATCHED OVER.
YOUR MOTHERS' LIVES WERE GIVEN IN SACRIFICE TO THAT VERY PURPOSE. ISHTAR AND OBATALA HAVE BEEN MERCIFUL.
OADIRA, YOU WILL BE ABLE TO COMMUNICATE WITH ALL LIFE IN THE SEAS. AAMIRA, YOU WILL SEE THROUGH THE EYES OF ANIMALS AND SPEAK WITH THEM.
YOU WILL ALL CONTROL THE ELEMENTS TO VARYING DEGREES. HEZIARA, YOU WILL COMMUNE WITH THE FOWL AND SPROUT YOUR WINGS ONCE MORE. YOU WILL FLY ABOVE AARDE.
I WILL...
FLY?

YOU WILL ALL DO SO MUCH MORE.

HERE ARE DOCUMENTS AND MAPS FOR EACH OF YOU. AS AGREED UPON WITH MADAME LALAURIE, NEZIKIAH AND I WILL VISIT EACH OF YOUR ESTATES IN THE COMING MONTHS FOR BREEDING.
INSTEAD OF THAT UNPLEASANT FARMING, I WILL HELP EACH OF YOU LEARN TO ACCESS YOUR ABILITIES AND HELP YOU ESCAPE. THE BRACELETS YOUR MOTHERS GAVE YOU WILL GUIDE YOUR JOURNEY.
THEY WILL BE A CONSTANT COMPANION AND HELP MAKE YOU AWARE OF EVERYTHING THAT IS HAPPENING AROUND YOU.
WITHOUT THEM, THERE IS NOWHERE SAFE FOR THE FOUR OF YOU EXCEPT SAHAEL. I MUST GO NOW, MY PRINCESSES. I WILL NEVER FORGET THIS MOMENT.
WAIT FOR ME AT YOUR ESTATES. IT MAY BE SOME YEARS BEFORE YOU SEE EACH OTHER AGAIN. I WILL SERVE YOU WHEN I CAN, BUT YOU MUST GET TO SAHAEL.
WHAT DO WE DO?
TRUE PRINCESSES? IT DOESN'T SEEM REAL. AND YET, SOLOMON'S WORDS BURN LIKE A HOT IRON IN MY MIND.
WILL WE TRULY BE FREE? WILL OUR PEOPLE TRULY BE FREE?

WELL, YOU THREE LOOK HAPPY. WHAT, DID NEZIKIAH SHOW YOU HIS--
MARTHA! SHOW SOME LEVEL OF DECORUM. I TAKE IT YOU'RE PLEASED WITH THE OUTCOME OF THE RUMBLE, OADIRA?
YES, MADAME. NÉZIKIAH IS A GOOD MAN. AND YOU ARE A GOOD MATRON.
INDEED. SAY FAREWELL TO YOUR COUSINS. IT WILL BE SOME TIME BEFORE YOU SEE EACH OTHER AGAIN...
IF EVER.
WE WILL SEE EACH OTHER AGAIN, SISTERS, ON THE SHORES OF SAHAEL.
WE WILL BE FREE. OUR PEOPLE WILL BE FREE.

WE WILL BE *FREE*. FOR THE FIRST TIME IN MY LIFE, I BELIEVE THAT STATEMENT. SOLOMON HAS CHANGED EVERYTHING.
I FEEL *POWER* GROWING INSIDE ME I'VE NEVER UNDERSTOOD. THE AIR FEELS DIFFERENT.
I FEEL *DIFFERENT*. I AM OF THE *ROYAL BLOODLINE*.
SAHAEL WILL BE *REDEEMED*.
I WILL BE FREE, AND I WON'T BE THE ONLY ONE.

SAHAEL

TEAM

DWAYNE A. MADRY
WRITER/CREATOR

STEVEN HEUMANN
ADAPTER

KEVIN WHITE
PRESIDENT

DAMON BOWIE
PENCILS/INKS/COLORS

JESSHAVOK
LETTERER/FORMATTING

FOLLOW US

www.SAHAEL.com

 @Sahaelian

 @TheBloodlinesOfSahael

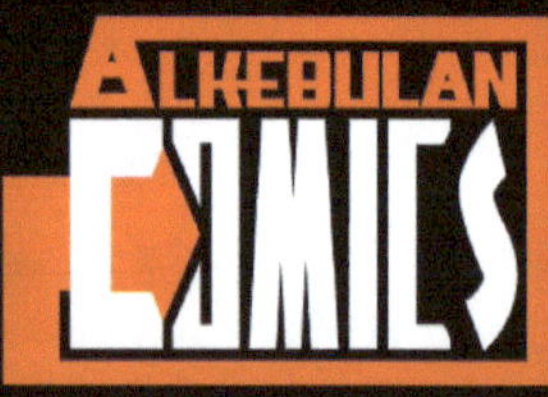

WRITER & CREATOR

IS A UTAH NATIVE WHO HAS A DEEP LOVE FOR HISTORY, SEEKS TO UNCOVER THE TRUTH HIDDEN BETWEEN THE LINES.

HIS MISSION IS TO CHALLENGE CONVENTIONAL NARRATIVES BY ADDRESSING UNCOMFORTABLE AND CONTROVERSIAL TOPICS, SPARKING RATIONAL THOUGHT RATHER THAN COGNITIVE DISSONANCE THROUGH HIS THOUGHT-PROVOKING CONTENT, CONCEPTS, AND QUESTIONS.

FROM A YOUNG AGE, DWAYNE FELT THE ABSENCE OF REPRESENTATION IN MEDIA AND DECIDED TO TAKE ACTION AT JUST 16 YEARS OLD. THIS LED TO THE CREATION OF THE WORLD OF SAHAEL, WHICH EXPLORES THE SCATTERING OF THE DIASPORA AND TELLS A UNIQUE AFRICAN-AMERICAN STORY THAT GOES BEYOND THE TYPICAL SLAVE NARRATIVE, FOCUSING ON THE ENSLAVED PEOPLE SENT FROM THEIR HOMELAND OF ALKEBULAN TO THE AMERICAS.

DWAYNE CURRENTLY RESIDES IN SALT LAKE CITY, UTAH, WITH HIS LOYAL DOG VALKYRIE.

SOCIETY OF SECRETS

NAIROHENGE

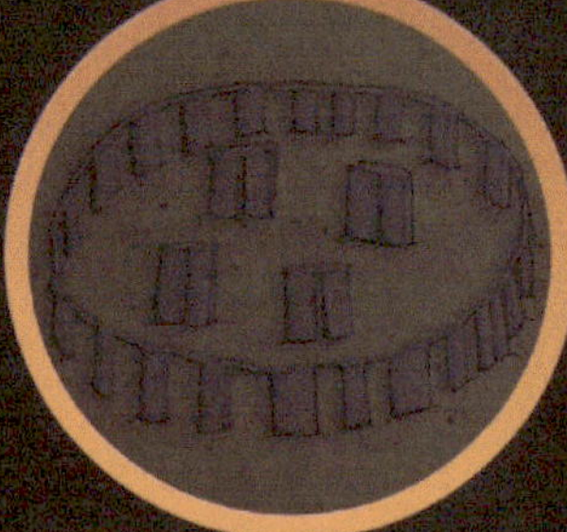
SAHAELAND

CENTRAL SAHAERION

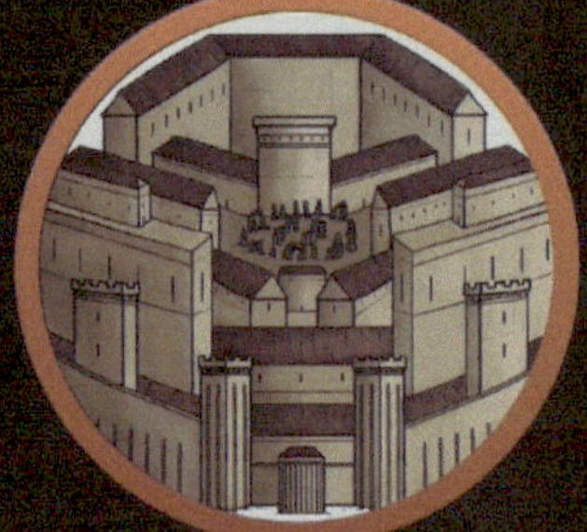
SAHAEDRON

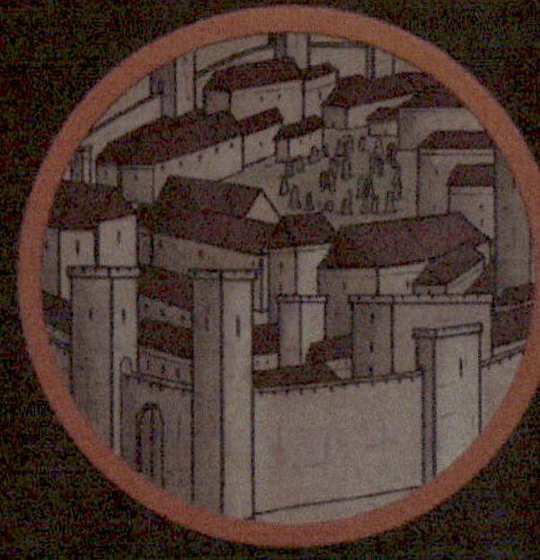
SAH

THE 'ARTH NATIONS
DALE ISLAND
AZTERA ISLAND
NARSA ISLAND
NISTIAN OCEAN
THE SOCIETY OF SECRETS
THRENDIEN ISLAND
ARUA ISLAND
NAHARIS'N REALM
BLADELAND ISLAND
NIGILD OCEAN
THE STATE'S OR
NIBIRU CASTLE
THE NIBIRU GATES
NIBIRU PALACE
INHERITANCE
THE ASH GATE OF NIGLOS
EBONY ISLAND

CITY
CITY (UNDER FLOUTING LAND)
PALACE / CASTLE / TEMPLE

AEL

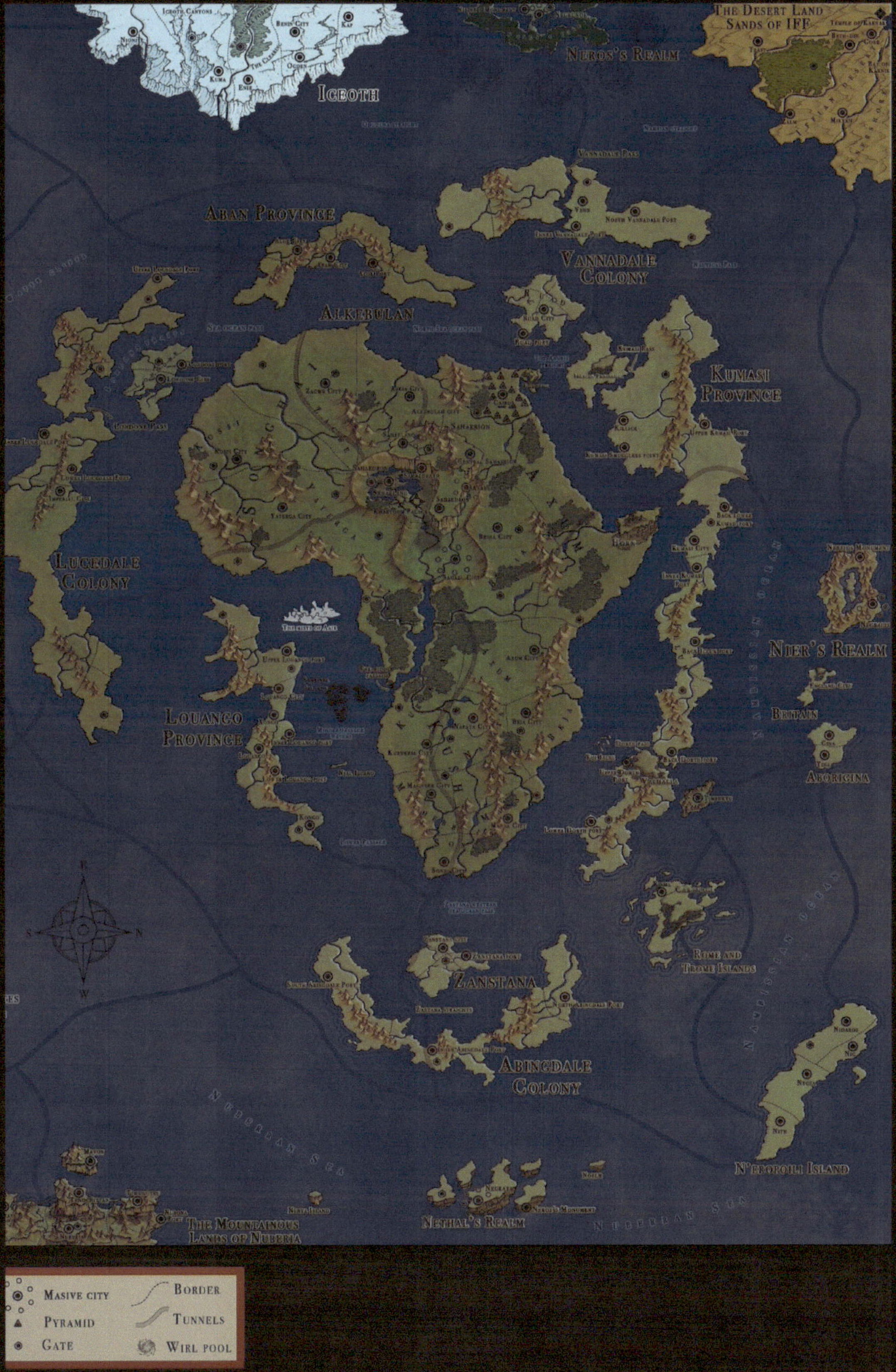

SAHADEATH

KHARTOUM PALACE

AARDIAN CITY

ALKEBULAN CITY

SAHAEL CITY

ICEOTH
NEROS'S REALM
THE DESERT LAND
SANDS OF IFE
ABAN PROVINCE
ALKEBULAN
VANNADALE COLONY
KUMASI PROVINCE
LUCEDALE COLONY
NIER'S REALM
LOUANGO PROVINCE
ZANSPANA
ABINGDALE COLONY
NETHAL'S REALM
THE MOUNTAINOUS LANDS OF NUBERIA
N'EKROPLI ISLAND
ABORIGINA
BRITAIN

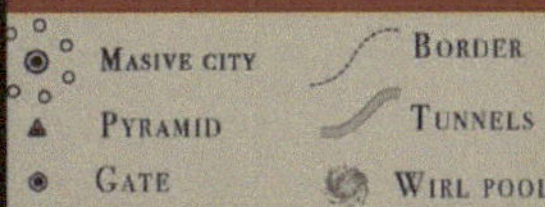

MASIVE CITY
PYRAMID
GATE
BORDER
TUNNELS
WIRL POOL

Nairostone Gate

The Lookout

WIR Palace

WIRU's Sanctuary

The Shaelian Passage

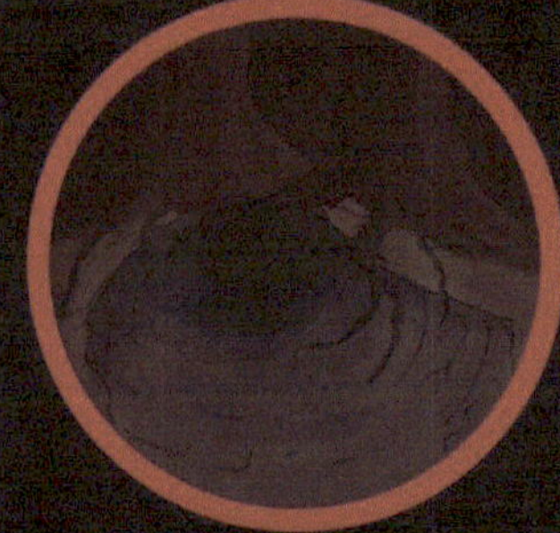

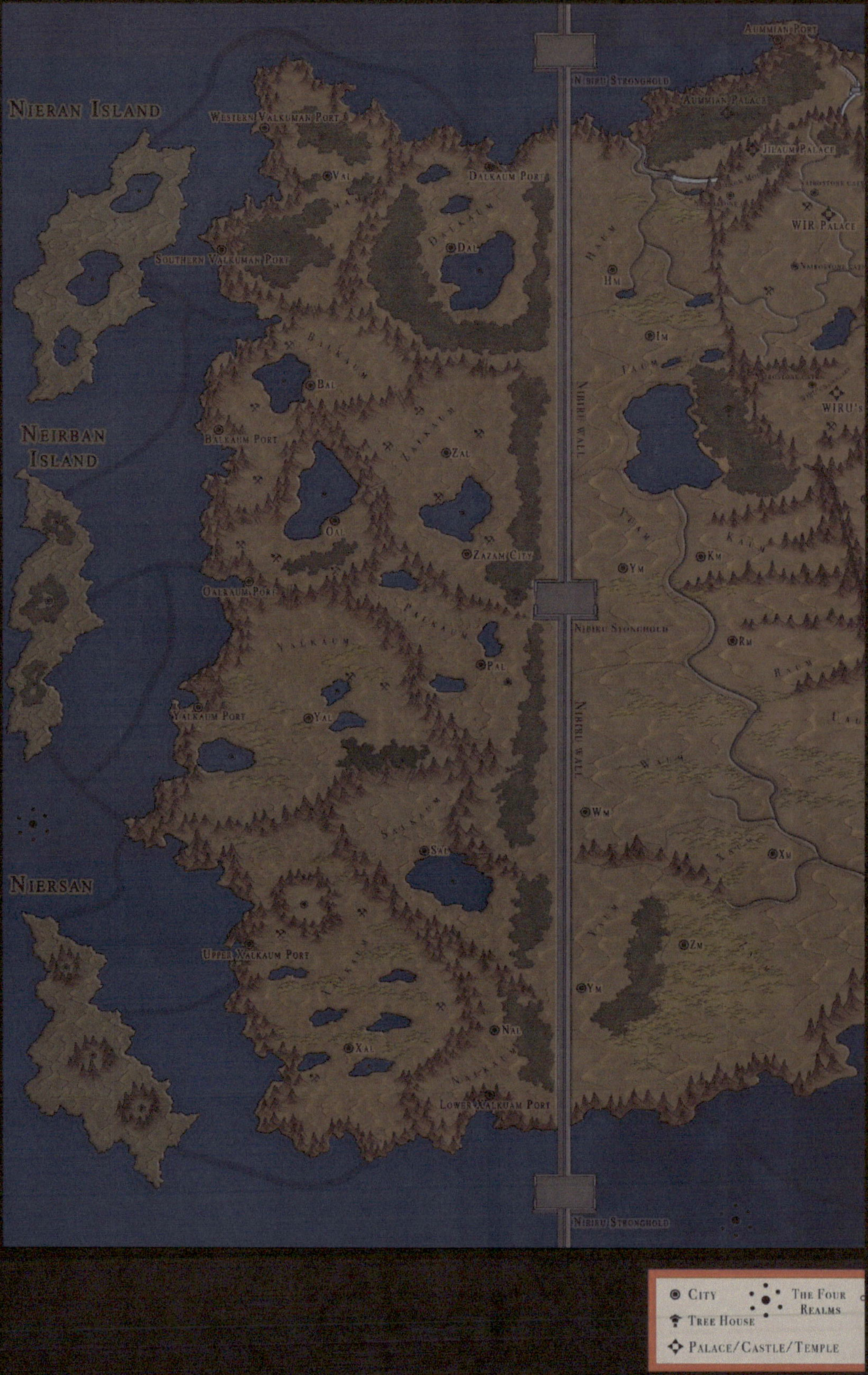

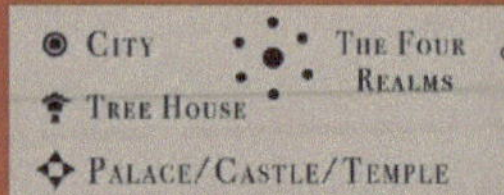

Aummian Port

Aummian Palace

The Stone Gate

Jilaum Palace

Carthage City

CHARACTER BIO:

NERGAL
THE HIGH QUEEN OF SAHAEL

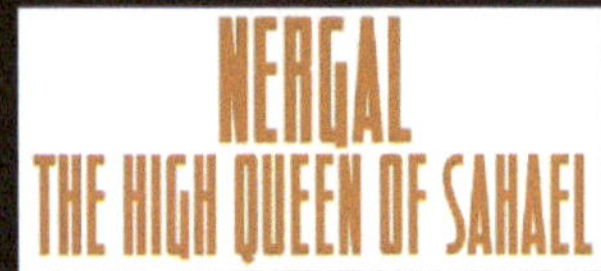

NERGAL, AS THE HIGH QUEEN OF SAHAEL, SHE NOT ONLY HOLDS THE MOST POWERFUL POSITION IN THE LAND, BUT ALSO BEARS THE IMMENSE RESPONSIBILITY OF SAFEGUARDING THE PROSPERITY AND SECURITY OF HER PEOPLE.

THE WELFARE OF EVERY SAHAELIAN, WHETHER RESIDING WITHIN THE BORDERS OF THE KINGDOM OR SCATTERED ACROSS THE DIASPORA, RESTS ON HER SHOULDERS. THE DIASPORA, A GROUP OF SAHAELIANS WHO WERE FORCIBLY REMOVED FROM THEIR HOMELAND BY THE TRINITY BEFORE NERGAL'S BIRTH, SERVES AS A CONSTANT REMINDER OF THE DARK AND TUMULTUOUS HISTORY OF SAHAEL.

THE DECISION TO SEPARATE THESE INDIVIDUALS FROM THEIR ROOTS WAS A CALCULATED MOVE BY THE TRINITY TO DISRUPT THE ANCIENT ORDER OF THE CHOSEN BLOODLINES, WHO HAVE LONG GOVERNED SAHAEL WITH WISDOM AND STRENGTH. DESPITE THE CHALLENGES AND OBSTACLES THAT COME WITH HER POSITION, NERGAL REMAINS RESOLUTE IN HER DUTY TO PROTECT AND UPHOLD THE LEGACY OF THE CHOSEN BLOODLINES.

WITH UNWAVERING DETERMINATION AND AN UNYIELDING SPIRIT, SHE SEEKS TO UNITE HER PEOPLE, BOTH WITHIN SAHAEL AND BEYOND ITS BORDERS, IN A COMMON PURSUIT OF PEACE, PROSPERITY, AND ***JUSTICE***.

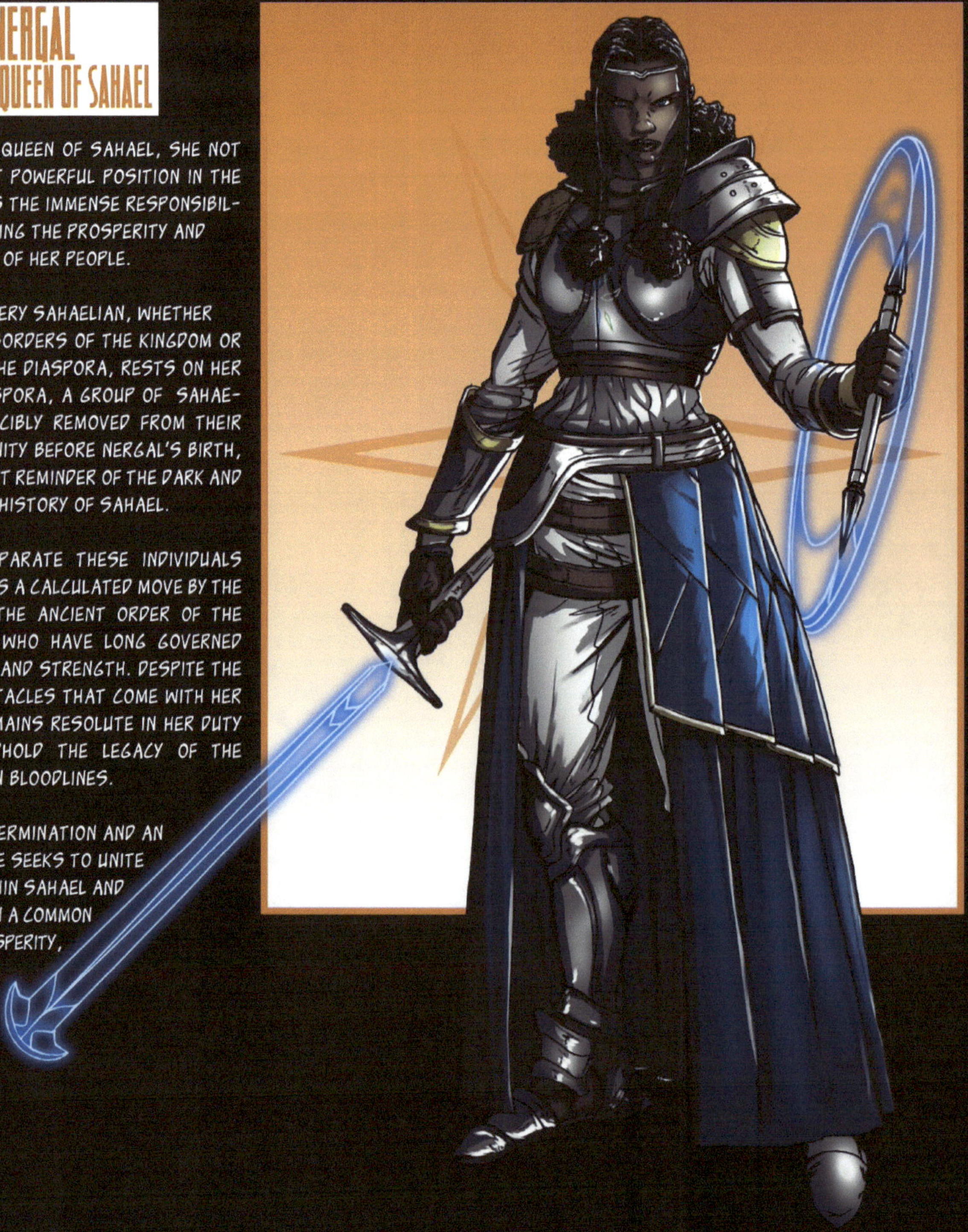

NINTI
THE GREAT QUEEN OF SAHAEL

NINTI, AS THE GREAT QUEEN OF SAHAEL, HOLDS A POSITION OF IMMENSE INFLUENCE AND AUTHORITY WITHIN THE KINGDOM, SECOND ONLY TO THE HIGH QUEEN HERSELF. HER PRIMARY RESPONSIBILITY IS TO SAFEGUARD THE WELL-BEING OF ALL SAHAELIANS, ENSURING THEIR SAFETY AND PROTECTION FROM ANY THREATS THAT MAY ARISE.

NINTI'S VIGILANT WATCH EXTENDS NOT ONLY TO THOSE WITHIN THE BORDERS OF SAHAEL BUT ALSO TO THE SCATTERED MEMBERS OF THE DIASPORA WHO WERE CRUELLY TAKEN FROM THEIR HOMELAND BY THE TRINITY BEFORE HER OWN BIRTH. THE DIASPORA, A GROUP OF SAHAELIANS WHO WERE FORCIBLY REMOVED FROM SAHAEL, SERVES AS A PAINFUL REMINDER OF THE DARK AND TUMULTUOUS HISTORY OF THE KINGDOM. THE TRINITY'S ACTIONS IN SEPARATING THESE INDIVIDUALS FROM THEIR ROOTS WERE A DELIBERATE ATTEMPT TO DISRUPT THE ANCIENT ORDER OF THE CHOSEN BLOODLINES, WHICH HAVE LONG SERVED AS THE FOUNDATION OF SAHAEL'S SOCIETAL STRUCTURE AND GOVERNANCE.

THE GOAL WAS TO WEAKEN THE POWER OF THE CHOSEN BLOODLINES AND PREVENT THE BIRTHS OF THE PROPHESIED BLACK MADONNA'S, WHO ARE BELIEVED TO POSSESS SIGNIFICANT INFLUENCE AND ABILITIES. NINTI'S QUEST TO LOCATE AND REUNITE THE DIASPORA IS DRIVEN BY A DEEP SENSE OF DUTY AND A PROFOUND DESIRE TO RESTORE UNITY AND STRENGTH TO SAHAEL.

THROUGH HER TIRELESS EFFORTS AND UNWAVERING DETERMINATION, SHE SEEKS TO NOT ONLY PROTECT HER PEOPLE FROM EXTERNAL THREATS BUT ALSO TO ENSURE THAT THE LEGACY OF THE CHOSEN BLOOD-LINES IS PRESERVED AND THAT THE POTENTIAL OF THE BLACK MADONNA'S IS NOT STIFLED.

IN HER ROLE AS THE GREAT QUEEN, NINTI STANDS AS A BEACON OF HOPE AND RESILIENCE FOR ALL SAHAE-LIANS, GUIDING THEM TOWARDS A FUTURE FILLED WITH PROMISE AND POSSIBILITY.

ARISHKEGAL
THE REGENT QUEEN OF SAHAEL

ARISHKEGAL, AS THE REGENT QUEEN OF SAHAEL, OCCUPIES THE THIRD MOST POWERFUL POSITION WITHIN THE KINGDOM, PLAYING A CRUCIAL ROLE IN SAFEGUARDING THE WELL-BEING AND INTERESTS OF SAHAELIANS BOTH WITHIN THE BORDERS OF SAHAEL AND ACROSS THE VAST EXPANSE OF AARDE.

HER RESPONSIBILITIES EXTEND BEYOND THE CONFINES OF THE KINGDOM, REACHING OUT TO THOSE WHO WERE TORN FROM THEIR HOMELAND AND SCATTERED ACROSS THE DIASPORA BY THE DESTRUCTIVE TRINITY INVASIONS THAT OCCURRED BEFORE HER BIRTH.

THE TRINITY'S CALCULATED ACTIONS IN SEPARATING THE MEMBERS OF THE DIASPORA FROM SAHAEL WERE PART OF A LARGER STRATEGY TO DISRUPT THE ANCIENT ORDER MAINTAINED BY THE CHOSEN BLOODLINES, WHO HAVE LONG SERVED AS PILLARS OF STRENGTH AND WISDOM IN SAHAELIAN SOCIETY.

THE INTENTION BEHIND THESE INVASIONS WAS TO WEAKEN THE POWER AND INFLUENCE OF THE CHOSEN BLOODLINES, THEREBY HINDERING THE PROPHESIED ARRIVAL OF THE BLACK MADONNA'S, WHO ARE BELIEVED TO POSSESS EXTRAORDINARY ABILITIES AND SIGNIFICANCE IN SAHAELIAN LORE. ARISHKEGAL'S ROLE AS THE REGENT QUEEN INVOLVES NAVIGATING THE COMPLEXITIES OF SAHAELIAN POLITICS AND DIPLOMACY, ENSURING THE CONTINUED PROSPERITY AND UNITY OF HER PEOPLE IN THE FACE OF EXTERNAL THREATS AND INTERNAL CHALLENGES.

HER COMMITMENT TO PROTECTING AND EMPOWERING THE SAHAELIANS, AS WELL AS THE SCATTERED MEMBERS OF THE DIASPORA, REFLECTS A DEEP SENSE OF DUTY AND LOYALTY TO THE KINGDOM AND ITS TRADITIONS.

THROUGH HER LEADERSHIP AND GUIDANCE, ARISHKEGAL STRIVES TO UPHOLD THE LEGACY OF THE CHOSEN BLOODLINES AND PAVE THE WAY FOR A FUTURE WHERE THE POTENTIAL OF THE BLACK MADONNA'S CAN BE REALIZED WITHOUT INTERFERENCE OR OBSTACLES. IN HER POSITION AS THE REGENT QUEEN, SHE STANDS AS A BEACON OF STRENGTH AND RESILIENCE, INSPIRING HOPE AND UNITY AMONG ALL SAHAELIANS, NO MATTER WHERE THEY MAY RESIDE ON AARDE.

MORRIGHAN
THE QUEEN OF SAHAEL

MORRIGHAN, THE ALBINO QUEEN OF SAHAEL, OCCUPIES THE FOURTH MOST POWERFUL POSITION WITHIN THE KINGDOM, WIELDING INFLUENCE AND AUTHORITY TO ENSURE THE WELL-BEING AND PROSPERITY OF SAHAELIANS RESIDING IN THE FOUR CITIES OF SAHAEL.

DESPITE HER UNIQUE APPEARANCE AND STANDING WITHIN SAHAELIAN SOCIETY, MORRIGHAN PLAYS A VITAL ROLE IN UPHOLDING THE TRADITIONS AND VALUES THAT HAVE DEFINED THE KINGDOM FOR GENERATIONS. ONE OF MORRIGHAN'S PRIMARY RESPONSIBILITIES INVOLVES ACTIVE PARTICIPATION IN THE SAHAELIAN CONGRESS, A GOVERNING BODY THAT OVERSEES IMPORTANT DECISIONS AND POLICIES AFFECTING THE KINGDOM AS A WHOLE.

THROUGH HER INVOLVEMENT IN THE CONGRESS, MORRIGHAN WORKS TIRELESSLY TO ADDRESS THE NEEDS OF SAHAELIANS ACROSS THE FOUR CITIES, ADVOCATING FOR THEIR RIGHTS AND ENSURING THAT THEIR VOICES ARE HEARD IN MATTERS OF GOVERNANCE AND POLICY-MAKING. THE ISSUE OF THE DIASPORA, THE GROUP OF SAHAELIANS FORCIBLY TAKEN FROM THEIR HOMELAND BY THE TRINITY BEFORE MORRIGHAN'S BIRTH, REMAINS A PRESSING CONCERN FOR THE ALBINO QUEEN.

THE DELIBERATE ACT OF SEPARATING THE MEMBERS OF THE DIASPORA FROM SAHAEL WAS A CALCULATED MOVE TO DISRUPT THE ANCIENT ORDER OF THE CHOSEN BLOODLINES AND PREVENT THE EMERGENCE OF THE PROPHESIED BLACK MADONNA'S, WHO ARE BELIEVED TO POSSESS SIGNIFICANT POWER AND INFLUENCE. MORRIGHAN'S INVOLVEMENT IN LOCATING AND REUNITING THE DIASPORA REFLECTS HER COMMITMENT TO PRESERVING THE UNITY AND STRENGTH OF SAHAELIAN SOCIETY.

BY WORKING DILIGENTLY TO ADDRESS THE LEGACY OF THE TRINITY INVASIONS AND RESTORE THE BONDS BETWEEN SAHAELIANS ACROSS AARDE, MORRIGHAN STRIVES TO UPHOLD THE TRADITIONS OF THE CHOSEN BLOODLINES AND ENSURE THAT THE POTENTIAL OF THE BLACK MADONNA'S IS NOT LOST TO HISTORY. AS THE ALBINO QUEEN OF SAHAEL, MORRIGHAN STANDS AS A SYMBOL OF RESILIENCE AND DETERMINATION, GUIDING HER PEOPLE TOWARDS A FUTURE WHERE UNITY, PROSPERITY, AND THE LEGACY OF THE CHOSEN BLOODLINES ARE UPHELD WITH HONOR AND RESPECT. HER PRESENCE IN THE SAHAELIAN CONGRESS AND HER EFFORTS.

THE ORISHAN FAMILY TREE